For Michel, who loved this story
LB

For Marie-France and Georges and the little red tractor we knew
when we were little
DM

MYRIAD BOOKS LIMITED
35 Bishopsthorpe Road, London SE26 4PA

First published in 1999 by
MIJADE PUBLICATIONS
16-18, rue de l'Ouvrage 5000 Namur-Belgium

© Laurence Bourguignon, 1999
© Dominique Maes, 1999
Translation Lisa Pritchard

ISBN 1 905606 25 7

Printed in China

MAX

the little red tractor

Laurence Bourguignon
Dominique Maes

MYRIAD BOOKS LIMITED

Max the tractor could see the end of the assembly line. He was very proud of his shiny red paint. He was nearly ready!

"I hope someone will come and buy me very soon," he said to himself. "I can't wait to start working in the fields!"

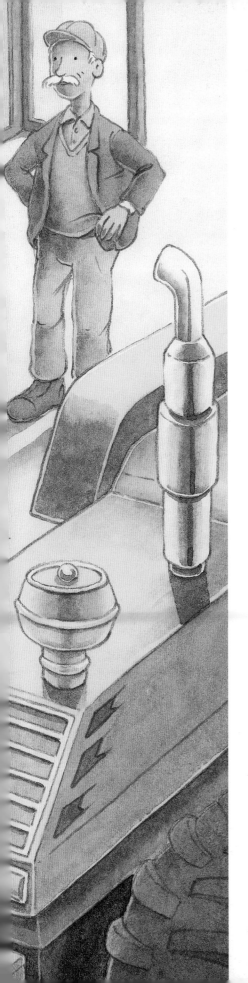

But when he got to the shop the other tractors were
in no hurry to be sold. They thought he was silly.
They were snug and warm, and someone polished them every day.

Max didn't want to wait. "I do hope someone buys me soon and
takes me to their farm."

Every time a customer came in, Max would beep his horn to make
sure they noticed him.

One happy day, Max's dream came true. Mr McDonald
came in and said, "I'll have that lovely red tractor please."

Max was thrilled. He trundled up onto the big lorry,
put his brakes on and away they went – OFF TO THE FARM!

That night Max slept in
the barn. It was very
noisy – there were pigs,
chickens and ducks, and
even a wheezy old Jeep.
Max didn't sleep very
well at all.

Next morning Max was surprised. Everyone on the farm got up very early!
At eight o'clock Mr McDonald climbed into Max's cab.
"Come on, sleepyhead, let's see what you can do," he said.

Grumbling a little, Max started his engine and they set off. He wondered where they were going. It seemed a very long way.

The farmer turned into a field. Max was horrified when he saw how big it was – and how muddy it was.

"Oh my goodness," he said to himself. "He can't expect me to go in there. MY SHINY RED PAINT WILL GET ALL DIRTY!"

Max ploughed the field all day, up and down, back and forth. As he trundled along, Max thought about the lovely warm, clean shop where all the other tractors still stood. He wasn't sure he wanted to work in the fields after all.

Still, never mind. He revved his engine, flashed his lights and set off once again.

That evening, when Max drove into the barn, the old Jeep wheezed: "Did you have a good day?"

"I'm exhausted," said Max, "but we got a lot done."

The weeks went by. Max worked in all weathers, through heavy rain and strong winds.

He knew the wheat and barley had to be planted…

The fences had to be mended, and the cows had to have water.

Sometimes on his way home he paused to look at the fields.
Everything looked perfect. The wheat was growing and all was well.

Max realised that he was happy.

Mr McDonald was happy too. "The wheat looks really good this year," he smiled. "It will be a good harvest. You've done well, Max."

Max blushed.

In August Max met a beautiful yellow combine harvester.
She was amazingly strong. He really liked working with her –
they made a good team!

Later a mean green machine came to pull up the sugarbeet. It was very clumsy. Sometimes it even bumped into Max. He was sure it did that on purpose.

By the time all the harvest was in, Max's exhaust pipe was wonky and his right headlamp hurt.

The farmer sighed. "I'll have to take you back to the shop."

When Max heard that, he started to SHAKE. He didn't want to go back to the store. He wanted to stay on the farm.

Mr McDonald parked Max in front of the shop and went in. Max shivered:
"It looks so dark, I don't want to go in there," he whispered sadly.

But when Mr McDonald came out of the shop, Max wasn't sad any more! HE WAS GOING TO BE REPAIRED!

When Max got back to the farm he felt like singing and dancing but he didn't know how to. So he settled for beeping his horn and flashing his headlights.

And what was that soft white stuff in the air? Max sighed happily. He was home and all was well.